A Transportation Tale by

# TOM ANGLEBERGER

Pictures by

# JOHN HENDRIX

This book is dedicated to my amazing great-aunts, Ethel and Grace Angleberger. —T.A.

To my dad, who taught me how to work hard with a smile (and also how to mow). —J.H.

THE ILLUSTRATIONS IN THIS BOOK WERE MADE WITH PEN AND INK WITH FLUID ACRYLIC WASHES ON STRATHMORE BRISTOL VELLUM.

Library of Congress Cataloging-in-Publication Data  Angleberger, Tom.  McToad mows Tiny Island / by Tom Angleberger ; illustrated by John Hendrix.  pages cm  Summary: Every Thursday, as a break from mowing Big Island, McToad and his tractor make their way to Tiny Island, using various modes of transportation and types of machinery to get there and back.  ISBN 978-1-4197-1650-8
[1. Transportation–Fiction. 2. Vehicles–Fiction. 3. Machinery–Fiction. 4. Mowing machines–Fiction.] I. Hendrix, John, 1976- illustrator. II. Title.  PZ7.A585Mct 2015  [E]–dc23  2014041033

Text copyright © 2015 Tom Angleberger. Illustrations copyright © 2015 John Hendrix. Book design by John Hendrix and Chad W. Beckerman.

Abrams Books for Young Readers are available at special discounts when purchased in quantity for premiums and promotions as well as fundraising or educational use.  Special editions can also be created to specification. For details, contact specialsales@abramsbooks.com or the address below.

ABRAMS
THE ART OF BOOKS SINCE 1949

115 West 18th Street
New York, NY 10011
www.abramsbooks.com

# McTOAD MOWS TINY ISLAND

ABRAMS BOOKS FOR YOUNG READERS

NEW YORK

McToad likes Thursdays.

Every other day of the week he mows the grass on . . .

BIG ISLAND

But Thursday is the day
he mows . . .

TINY
ISLAND

First, McToad rides his lawn mower out of the shed.

Then he drives it up into the back of a big

TRUCK.

The truck takes the lawn mower to a

# TRAIN.

# A Forklift

puts the lawn mower onto the train.

The train takes the lawn mower to the airport.

A conveyor belt carries
the lawn mower to an
**AIRPLANE.**

The airplane flies to the other side of Big Island.

A
# BAGGAGE BUGGY
takes the lawn mower to a
# HELICOPTER.

The helicopter picks up the lawn mower and flies to the

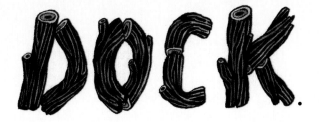

DOCK.

A big rope lowers the lawn mower to the deck of a boat.

The
# BOAT
sails across the ocean to Tiny Island.

A

# CRANE

lowers the lawn mower onto the island.

# McTOAD
## MOWS
## TINY
## ISLAND.

McToad pauses. He drinks a glass of lemonade.
He puts a little oil in the lawn mower.

McToad finishes mowing Tiny Island.

Then . . .

The **CRANE** lifts the lawn mower onto the **BOAT**,

which sails across the ocean to the **DOCK**, where the

**HELICOPTER** picks it up and flies it to the airport just in

time for the **Baggage Buggy** to get it to the **AIRPLANE**,

which zooms it across Big Island to the conveyor belt, which takes it

to the **Forklift**, which loads it on the **TRAIN** that goes

to the station, where the **TRUCK** is ready to take it home.

McToad rides the lawn mower back into the shed.
And wipes it down with a nice, clean cloth.

McToad likes Thursdays.